Mary Hoffman writes: "I've been making up stories for children for over 20 years and have now written more than 50 books. These four

stories ... baby Emily - ... re still quite yo... So they are full of things that were ... ... family life at the time: trips to the zoo, picnics outdoors and in, attempts to buy swimsuits in summer and choosing a pet (though in our case it was always a cat).

I spend a lot of time visiting schools and meeting children and I get letters from readers all over the world. My favourite was from a 12-year-old girl, who said she learned to read from a book of mine. That was BEWARE PRINCESS!

Other favourites of mine are AMAZING GRACE, MY GRANDMOTHER HAS BLACK HAIR and HENRY'S BABY, which are all about children I've made up, but who seem very real to me. I like books which you can read more than once and find something different in them each time. With the help of Leon Baxter's pictures, that's what I have tried to ... ...e.

First published in Great Britain in 1987
by Macdonald and Co. (Publishing) Ltd

Published in Great Britain in 1994 by

 Belitha Press Ltd
London House, Great Eastern Wharf,
Parkgate Road, London SW11 4 NQ

Reprinted 1997

British Library Cataloguing in Publication Data for this book
is available from the British Library.

Printed in Hong Kong

ISBN 1 85561 287 9 (hardback)
ISBN 1 85561 747 1 (paperback)

Mary Hoffman

A Fine Picnic

illustrated by Leon Baxter

Belitha Press

Our family likes picnics.
Last Sunday we were all
getting ready for a picnic,
when, suddenly . . .

It rained! Oh no!
Our basket was packed.
Our flasks were full.
We were all ready.

'Come along,' said Mum. 'We're not going to let a little bit of rain spoil our picnic. Let's go.'

'Let's climb this hill and see what's at the top,' said Dad.

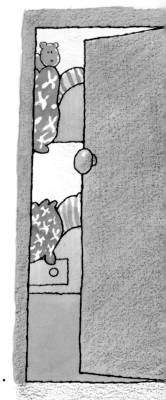

I stopped to pick flowers
on the way.
'Hurry up, Jack,' Mum called.

'This looks a good spot,' said Dad.
'Come on,' said Jess, 'I'm starving!'

'Lovely,' said Mum.
'Let's sit on the grass
and unpack the picnic.'
She spread out the cloth.

We had a lovely lunch
with crisps and sausages and bananas.
Some horses came up to see
what we were eating.
They wanted my cheese roll.

Our dog, Dallas, chased the rabbits.
He always does that sort of thing
on picnics.

After lunch we wanted to explore.
We left Mum and Dad with the baby
while we climbed
a bit further up the hill.

The view from the top was great.
And we met lots of bears.
It was very hot up there.

When we got back, the baby was
playing with the lambs.
She was giving them her crisps.
'What a lot of crumbs,' said Mum.
'Never mind,' said Dad.
'The birds will come and eat them.'

'Time to pack up,' said Mum.
'Mind you don't leave
any litter behind!'

'Wasn't it nice without
wasps and flies?' I said.
'Mind that bee!' said Jess.

'That was a great picnic,' I said,
'one of our best.'
'Yes,' said Mum, 'it was a fine day
for a picnic!'